"I was born in London in 1946 and grew up in a sweet shop in Essex. For several years I worked as a graphic designer, but in 1980 I decided to concentrate on writing and illustrating books for children.

My wife, Annette, and I have two grown-up children, Ben and Amanda, and we have put down roots in Suffolk.

I haven't recently counted how many books there are with my name on the cover but Percy the Park Keeper accounts for a good many of them. I'm reliably informed that they have sold more than three million copies. Hooray!

I didn't realise this when I invented Percy, but I can now see that he's very like my mum's dad, my grandpa. I even have a picture of him giving a ride to my brother and me in his old home-made wooden wheelbarrow!"

NICK BUTTERWORTH

# PERCY'S FRIEND
# THE BADGER

# NICK BUTTERWORTH

TED SMART

*Thanks Graham Daldry. You're a wizard.*

*Thanks Atholl McDonald. You're a hero!*

This edition produced for The Book People Ltd, Hall Wood Avenue, Haydock, St Helens WA11 9UL

1 3 5 7 9 10 8 6 4 2

ISBN: 0 00 770015 6

Text and illustrations copyright © Nick Butterworth 2002
The author asserts the moral right to be identified as the author of the work.

The HarperCollins website address is: www.harpercollins.co.uk

Printed and bound in China

# MY FRIEND THE BADGER

The badger is very strong and quite brave.

In some ways, he is a bit like an older brother to the other animals who live in the park.

He is always willing to lend a hand and he likes to share a joke. Like this one he told me yesterday... now what was it? I just can't remember it at the moment...

The badger's favourite thing in the whole world is digging. Sometimes, after a day of digging, he gets very dirty. What a pity that the worst thing in the world for the badger is having to have a bath.

Now what was that joke he told me? It will come to me in a minute...

One windy November, the
badger noticed that a
scarecrow, who had been
standing in a field next to
the park, had blown over.
The badger decided to stand
in for him and take the scarecrow's place.
Poor badger. He was out there
all night and got rather stiff.

It was a very thoughtful thing to do, and just the sort of thing the badger would do.

I wonder why he didn't just stand the scarecrow up again.

# THE BADGER REALLY LIKES . . .

Singing! He does two different kinds.
In tune and out of tune. Both loudly.

Anything black and white. Especially
animals. He thought this stripy towel
made him look like a zebra.

# THE BADGER DOESN'T LIKE . . .

Wet weather. He certainly doesn't like to be
out in it. It's too much like taking a shower.

Fizzy drinks. He says they fizz up his nose.
He'd rather have a banana milk shake.

Now what do you think of this? When the badger plays hide-and-seek, he will sometimes carry a mouse with him as a passenger.

He says he likes to help the smaller animals to join in. Well, he is very kind.

But sometimes I wonder if there might be another reason.

All I know is that the mice are extremely good at spotting things. And the badger usually wins.

Aha! I've just remembered that joke! Why do you put bulbs in the ground? So the worms can see where they're going!

I've got lots of pictures in my photo album.

A pullover from
Auntie Joyce.
I did tell him
it wouldn't fit.
It didn't fit
me either.
What a shame.

When he
goes walking,
the badger
likes to take
a friend
with him.

Here are some I took of my good friend, the badger.

Playing 'Shadows.'
Guess who!
He's making a
shadow of a
famous statue
he saw on a post
card in my hut.

The badger is
right-handed—
except for
toasted buns.
Then he uses
both hands.

I had a pleasant surprise one day, when the badger came knocking at my door to ask if he could hang up my washing for me.

I had an even bigger surprise when I saw
how he had hung it up! The badger and three
rabbits were having a fine time playing at
being pirates. Still, they did help to wash it
all through again. Well, the badger did.

# THE BADGER'S LIST

An old brown boot
A wooden flute
A model car
An empty jar
A nail
A snail
A rusty pail
A smelly bone
A telephone

A rubber tyre
A length of wire
A watering can
A frying pan
A screw
A shoe
A tin kazoo
A lacy shawl
A punctured ball

A crumbling brick
A walking stick
A twisted twig
A china pig
A lock
A sock
A cuckoo clock
A piece of string
A knobbly thing

A buckled wheel
A glockenspiel
A wooden boat
That wouldn't float
A mug
A plug
A Toby jug
A nest of ants
A pair of pants

You'd be amazed
You'd stop and stare
You'd be wide-eyed
And gasp for air
If you saw what
    the badger found
      When he was
        digging in the
        ground.

# FAVOURITE PLACES

I can't think of anyone who has more energy
than the badger. He loves to go for long
walks and all his favourite places are on the
edge of the park.

There's a rather lonely spot, where the wood
joins onto farmland, that I know he loves.
Sometimes he takes the mole up there and
they have a wonderful time together, digging
all day.

The badger has another favourite place
which is actually just outside the park. I
don't think he knows that I know about it.

It's an old barn which stands on some high ground. The badger likes to look out of the top window in the hay loft at the countryside all around. I expect it makes him feel like an explorer gazing out over distant lands.

Did I say all his favourite places were on the edge of the park? Well, of course, there is one that isn't. That's the big tree house where he lives with everyone else...

Here he is, my friend the badger, enjoying the view across the lake. I don't know who that model yacht belongs to, but I can tell you about the rubber duck...It's mine!

# Read all the stories about Percy and his animal friends...

Percy toys and videos
are also available.